# TANGLES

## Legend OR Loser

written by

# JACK BRAND

drawings by **Tom Jellett**

ALLEN&UNWIN
SYDNEY · MELBOURNE · AUCKLAND · LONDON

To my awesome kids, Ali, Tom and Hari,
who are my constant joy and inspiration.

First published in 2015

Allen & Unwin
83 Alexander Street
Crows Nest NSW 2065
Phone: (61 2) 8425 0100
Email: info@allenandunwin.com
Web: www.allenandunwin.com

A Cataloguing-in-Publication entry is available from the
National Library of Australia
www.trove.nla.gov.au

ISBN 978 1 76011 034 5

Cover and text design by Liz Seymour
Cover and internal illustrations by Tom Jellett
Set in Dyslexie 9/15 pt by Liz Seymour
This book was printed in Australia in August 2015 at McPherson's Printing Group,
76 Nelson St, Maryborough, Victoria 3465, Australia.

This title has been specifically styled in Dyslexie – a revolutionary font in which each
character has a unique form designed to simplify life for those who have dyslexia.
For more information about Dyslexie, go to dyslexiefont.com.

10 9 8 7 6 5 4 3 2 1

I really hurt myself **bad** this time.

'Banged up good and proper,' is what my dad said.

'Look at you, lad, you're a **mess**!'

And I am. If you could see my face you would know just how smashed up I am ... oh wait! You **can** see it ...

I want to eat lollies until I get sick too

Me too

And it really hurts to smile, but I can't help it because all my friends are sitting around my table laughing and cheering and Mum has put out so much food, including my favourite drink, lemon punch! Everyone's laughing about that, after what happened to my face.

'Want some more punch, Freddy?'

'Had enough punch, thanks, Cooper.'

Scabs plunges his hands into a bowl. 'I'm going to eat these lollies until I get sick!'

I have had the most amazing day.

But before I tell you about my amazing day, I should introduce myself.

My name is Frederick Augustus Reginald Tangles.

Kind of long, isn't it, and a bit embarrassing. I can't even spell it right half the time.

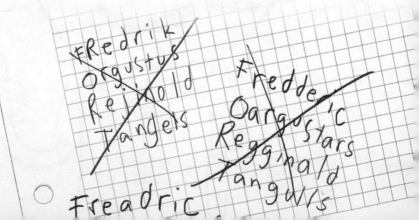

Luckily, most people just call me Freddy, or Freddy Tangles, which isn't embarrassing, unless they add something to it like,

# Freddy, your fly is down!

Or,

# Freddy Tangles! Did you just eat your snot?

Or,

**Freddy, do you want to play with my dollies?**

That last one is my little sister, Jessica. We share a bedroom and I don't mind playing with her and her dollies ... I just wish she wouldn't ask when I have friends over. She only does it to embarrass me.

And she can be scary too, like if she says, 'I've got lumps in my bottom,' don't ask, just run, because the lumps in her bottom are farts!

Did you hear that?

I think we should run too

I also have a dog called Mince. He's old and grumpy, though sometimes he forgets he's old and he jumps about like a puppy.

My dad is pretty much the same as Mince.

They even look the same.

My best
friend is
Blocker.

I haven't known him very long. His family is from Russia and he knows really cool Russian sayings like,

'A fly cannot enter a closed mouth.'

He says that when I talk too much. Most people just tell me to stop blabbering or something worse, but Blocker says, 'A fly cannot enter a closed mouth.'

I think that's pretty cool and also useful information.

Sometimes I talk too much on purpose just so he'll say it. He also says,

'Do not make an elephant out of a fly.'

He says that when I get mad.

Blocker and I have been best friends ever since I saved his life.

I really did!

I was outside my house kicking dog biscuits to Mince.

6

We play it all the time. I pretend I'm kicking goals for my team and Mince is the goalkeeper. Only goalkeepers don't usually swallow the ball when they save one.

Mince and I were playing when I saw this kid, who I later found out was Blocker, being hassled by a big person down the street.

The big person was grabbing him by his clothes and messing with his hair, and Blocker's voice was all high and whiny, saying, 'Stop it, stop, get off me!'

I decided that I had to help him, so I went over and said, 'Hey, leave him alone!' But the big person just pointed a big finger in my face and growled, 'You stay out of it!'

And it seemed like good advice, like what could a kid my size do anyway? But then I saw the answer to my question. It was staring me straight in the face.

I snuck up behind the big person, reached out and yanked on their pants. They flew down!

And there I was, staring at the **biggest** pair of pink undies I'd ever seen.

So easy! It was a great distraction. Blocker escaped, and the big person, well, you never heard someone scream like that.

It was all a bit scary but also funny. Actually, it was really funny, especially the way the big person ran off pulling their pants back up.

Blocker and I have been best friends ever since, even though it turns out that maybe I didn't save his life.

Should we help him?

You do know you're an ant, don't you?

Like I know I said I did and it really felt like I did, but ... Look, it's not my fault. It isn't! I didn't know what she looked like!

As it turned out, the person I dakked was his mum!

# I know ... I DAKKED HIS MUM!

Then Block invited me over to his house and like, no way was I ever going over there!

His mum would go nuts at me for sure. Block told me not to worry. He said that his mum loved Russian sayings and her favourite one of all time was,

*Even the Tsar needs to wear clothes.*

# DON'T WORRY?!

Don't worry when her favourite saying was about wearing clothes?!

I was pretty sure that if Blocker's mum thought this Tsar person needed to wear clothes, then she would think that she needed to wear clothes too!

I thought Blocker's mum must hate me and there was no way I was going over to his house, ever. I was telling Block all this, and how I was going to have to leave my own home and live in a cave because my mum was going to find out for sure, when he shoved his finger right in my mouth and said, 'A fly cannot enter a closed mouth.'

I've got to say that sticking a finger in someone's mouth really stops them from talking. I stopped talking straight away, like no way could a fly get in.

Blocker explained that a Tsar is a Russian king and the saying means that good manners are essential, so even the king has to wear clothes.

That was why Blocker's mum was out on the street in the first place. She was making Block tuck his shirt in and fix his hair, because that's good manners.

As it turned out, Blocker's mum was nice. She totally forgave me. And like, sure, whenever she answers the front door for me she backs away as if

10

I'm going to dak her again, but that's only natural because she's like, scarred for life.

You ever had a pet?

Had a pet worm once ... but my friends ate it

Apart from that, we get on famously. All I have to say is, 'Can I have another drink, **PLEASE?'** Or, 'Can I have another cookie, **PLEASE?'** And she nearly always gives it to me, saying how much my manners are improving.

Blocker's not my only friend though. I meet with the old gang at the park after school. Our other friends aren't allowed to go to the park without their parents because their parents think it's too dangerous. Which is so wrong.

My mum lets me go to the park all the time without her. Sometimes she thinks it's **SO** important that I go to the park on my own that she yells it at me.

**'Get out, OUT! GET OUT AND GO TO THE PARK NOW!!!'**

I think she lets me go on my own because she knows how responsible and mature I am.

And because I'm so mature I can look after all the other kids in the park who don't have their parents there to look after them.

That's a big responsibility, because there's nearly always someone in the park who needs looking after. Like my friend Kevin Ambleside. We call him Scabs because he's always got scabs on his knees and elbows and even his face from falling over all the time.

# This is Scabs.

I think the best falling over Scabs ever did was when he fell off his bike as usual, stood up, took one step and fell over again, only to stand up again and have this really big branch fall off the tree above him and land on his head.

# It was so funny.

At least it was funny until the branch fell on his head. He had to go to hospital after that.

Anyway, when he came back he had this really big scab on the top of his head where they had to shave off some of his hair to put stitches in. It looked really gross. You could see bits of dried blood and lumps between the stitches.

Tabitha Henry is in the park a lot too.

We call her Tabby. She's really smart and I like her a lot, even if she does disagree with me all the time.

She's always saying, 'Would you rather be a blah blah or a blah blah?'

For instance, when Scabs was carried away by the ambulance, Tabby asked, 'Would you rather have a tree branch fall on your head or get a needle?'

She asked that because the ambulance person gave Scabs a needle and while he was getting

I like scabs

Especially the oozy ones

it he was going **ouch ouch** because the needle hurt so much, but when the tree fell on him he didn't say *ouch* at all. He just lay there all quiet.

I said I would rather have the tree fall on me. Like, even though it knocked him out, he did get to ride in an ambulance, and no-one would ever actually choose to have a needle if they didn't have to.

Of course, Tabby chose to have the *needle*.

I said, 'Have you ever been chased by a bee?'

She said *yes*, and I said, 'So why did you run?' She said, 'Because they sting you,' so I said, 'Yeah, and it only has a tiny stinger. Imagine getting stung by a bee with a stinger the size of a needle!'

That's how much needles hurt.

She was about to disagree. I knew she was because she always does, but then something worse than needles happened.

I touched Tabby's tongue with my tongue.

15

This little kid dropped his ice cream on the ground right in front of us. When he tried to pick it up his mum wouldn't let him because it was dirty, so the kid ran off crying.

I had to act fast because our family has a ten-second rule, like if something falls on the ground it can still be eaten if it hasn't been there for more than ten seconds.

Time was running out so I snatched it up, but Tabby wanted it too because her family has the same rule, only their rule is a twenty-second rule, which is gross!

Imagine eating something that's been lying on the ground for like, fifteen seconds!

So we had to share it and we had to be quick because it was melting ...

... and that's when we touched tongues and, I have to say, I have never tasted anything so slimy and weird as Tabby's tongue.

That ice cream should have been ours

I hate the ten second rule

It was like licking a dead slug. Not that I've ever done that ... well okay, but that was a dare and I got five War Smackers and anyway, it was alive, not dead.

Tabby's tongue tasted so strange that I thought there might be something wrong with her.

When I got home I asked Jessica to stick her tongue out at me. She was only too pleased to do that.

When I tried to lick it to find out if her tongue tasted weird too, she wouldn't let me. She thought I was trying to get her back for the time we had a competition for the longest tongue and when I won she put dirt on my tongue.

Your tongue tastes like rotting worm!

Good, huh?

Mum wouldn't do it either, saying she didn't know where my tongue had been and like, it hadn't been anywhere.

The only person who would let me touch tongues with them was Mince. His tongue tasted okay. Quite nice really.

Anyway, I've started staring at the white wall in my bedroom for like hours without stopping and it's so cool!

And exciting.

What I do is, I sit in my chair and stare at the wall trying not to blink.

Did you know that if you stare at a white wall for long enough and want it bad enough, your eyes will start to shoot laser beams?

I swear it's true.

# LASER-BEAM EYES!

How cool is that?

I've been trying really hard with my staring but
I haven't started to shoot laser beams yet. I just need more time. I think maybe I'm blinking too much or not staring for long

enough, so my plan is to stare at the wall for an entire night without blinking.

When I do get my laser-beam power I'm going to use it for the good of all people of the Earth.

Like, for starters, I'm pretty sure my sister is evil so I'm planning to laser beam her ...

I'm not joking either, I really think she might be evil. It's only just happened, ever since she discovered a terrible secret about me ... I'm a deep sleeper!

It's turned her evil. Yesterday I woke up with salt in my eyes.

I've also woken up with a feather stuck up my nose! Another time there was water in my bed so it looked like I wet myself, and the worst time, I woke up with peanut butter on my fingers to make me think it was poo.

She thinks it's hilarious and I can't stop her because I'm asleep!

She's not the only evil thing I need to defeat with laser beams either. There's also this guy, Sid Malone.

He used to go to our school ... until he got expelled for fighting. I don't really remember him at school because he's older than us.

When he comes to the park with his gang we try to hide. He's already wrecked one of my skateboards and once he chucked my bike in a puddle. He also shoved Tabby over after she told him to go away. I told him that he shouldn't push people over and he came at me, but luckily some big person yelled, 'Oi! Malone, you leave those kids alone! Go pick on someone your own size!'

I'm just glad I wasn't his size.

Since then I've been extra scared of Sid because as he left he said, 'I'll get you later, Freddy dead-ee.'

That's what he said!

That's like the bully ants that chase us

You mean, bull ants

# Freddy dead-ee!

I remember Tabby once asking, 'What would you rather do, tell Sid Malone he smells or tell the principal he smells?'

That was easy. I would tell the principal.

Knowing that Sid might be after me is a big
worry, but it's nothing compared to what
happened after the worst day of my life.

And I mean the worst.

It started early.

I was playing with Mince and Jessica upstairs like
we always do before school when for no reason
Jessica started to cry. Only it wasn't normal
crying. It was so loud that the windows started
to rattle and people in cars out on the street
stopped and looked up
at our house, no
joke. I even heard
a tile slide off
our roof and
crash onto the
ground.

Now I don't
think I did
anything
particularly
bad.

# I didn't!

We were just playing a game, the same
game we'd played a hundred times before and she
never cried.

She started screaming,

# 'FREDDY KICKED ME!'

And it's true, I did kick her.

# BUT THAT WAS THE GAME!

We were playing Kick the Bug on My Bum. She kicked my bum after saying, 'Oh no, there's a fly on your bum, I'll kick it off.'

Then it was her turn and I said, 'Oh no, there's a cockroach on your bum.' And I kicked her!

Hardly worth freaking about!

Okay, so I did say she had a cockroach on her bum and she really does hate cockroaches but they ARE still

As a bug, I'm offended by this game

No respect

bugs so it was still allowed in the rules. No reason to go mental. And okay, I suppose I did say, 'Oh no, no really, there's five cockroaches right there and they're crawling all over your bum!'

And I suppose she didn't like it that I had to kick her bum five times, and I suppose I did throw a dead cockroach in her hair ...

Now I know that sounds pretty cruel of me but I couldn't take it anymore. Just that morning, while I was asleep, Jessica climbed up to the light fitting in our room, took it down and emptied the dead bugs inside it all over my face. She topped it off by putting a dead moth on my nose so when I woke up it looked like there was a monster moth attacking me. When I opened my mouth in surprise, heaps of little bugs dropped in.

So anyway, she chucked a massive spasm trying to get the cockroach out of her hair.

I got into trouble for that but it was nothing compared to what happened at school.

In class, the teacher gave Scarlett

Magnusson the job of calling the roll. Mr Brody hardly ever lets students do it, but he was busy so he gave it to Scarlett.

She was reading out our full names for fun ...

*Phillip Stephen Nguyen ...*
*Here!*

*Grace Seeyan Park ...*
*Here!*

*Robert Gregory Pickleberry ...*
*Here!*

People were laughing a bit at everyone's middle names and I knew that my name was next. I was a bit embarrassed because my full name is stupid, but Scarlett didn't read it out.

What's your name?

Worker Ant

Wow, that's the same as my name!

She just started laughing and said, 'Like, oh my god. That's so funny.'

Mr Brody said, 'Come on Scarlett, just finish the attendance, please.'

But she didn't. She picked up a black marker from Mr Brody's table, went to the whiteboard and said, 'I have got to show you this.'

And she wrote my whole name out on the board.

She wrote 'Frederick Augustus Reginald Tangles'.

Only she wrote it like this ...

Everyone started laughing because there on the board was the word FART.

Scarlett called out,
'**FARTBOY!**
Is **FARTBOY** here?'

Frederick
Augustus
Reginald
Tangles

I didn't answer because that wasn't my name. Some of the kids started pointing at me going, 'Yeah, there he is, there's **FARTBOY!**'

Mr Brody grabbed the whiteboard eraser and wiped at my name on the whiteboard but it wouldn't come off. He said, 'Oh Scarlett, you used the permanent marker. Oh well, we'll get that off at recess.'

# RECESS!

Before recess at least five other kids came into our class to deliver messages and they all laughed at the board. We also have a window on one side of our classroom that looks out onto a hall where kids walk past all the time. Word must have spread because heaps of kids came to the window to have a look.

By the time it was recess, the whole school was calling me FARTBOY.

And it's not that I don't like the word **fart**. It's a great word, one of my favourites for sure. Like, all I have to do is say fart or say, 'Uh-oh, I just farted,' and everyone laughs. Or if I change the words of a song, like if the words were 'Ooh yeah, I love you with all my heart', I can sing, 'Ooh yeah, I love you with all my fart', or 'I love to fart with all my heart', or 'I fart you with all my fart' and everyone laughs.

Fart was a great word because it made me funny, but now ... now everyone was laughing at **fart** but the fart was me!

# AND I MEAN EVERYONE!

I farted

That's disgusting! Hey, lets go eat that dead worm over there

It was nonstop. Everywhere I looked there was someone saying something about me being Fartboy.

So I stood near the teacher in the playground to stop everyone saying things, but Kathy Siddle still came up and said, right in front of the teacher, 'Hi, smelly Fartboy.'

The teacher raised her eyebrows at Kathy and said, 'That's not very nice, Kathy.'

And was I relieved, like, at last some help.

Then Kathy said, 'But his name is Frederick Augustus Reginald Tangles, and if you take the first letter of each name it spells FART.'

The teacher thought about that and said, 'Oh, so it does! F-A-R-T, fart, very good.'

# GOOD?

And off walked the teacher as if everything was okay.

So I'm left standing there next to Tabby, who says, 'What would you rather be, a Fartboy or a Burpgirl?'

Are you a boy or a girl?

Can't you tell?

I don't even know which I am!

Everyone said Burpgirl, even the boys.

So there I was, one Fartboy in a school full of Burpgirls. They were saying that burps don't smell so they would rather be a burp than a fart and I agreed, saying, 'I'm a Burpgirl too then,' but they wouldn't let me.

Mr Brody did manage to clean the whiteboard at last, but it was too late.

At lunch I was getting teased all the time. I asked Blocker what I should do and he said, 'In Russia they say: you cannot stop the river, it will flow as it chooses.'

I didn't have a clue what he was talking about. Like, what river?

Blocker explained, 'The flow of the river is the teasing words. You can't stop a river flowing, can you?'

'I suppose not.'

'Well, the teasing is the river.'

33

Whatever. At least Block stuck by me, even after someone said to him, 'You must like the smell of farts to sit next to him.' (This was actually almost true, because Blocker once told me that he liked the smell of his own farts.)

But that wasn't the point. The point was that

## I didn't smell like farts!

The whole thing was so stupid ... as stupid as my name!

When I got home I told Mum everything. I finished by saying, 'And it's all your fault!'

I told her that I wanted my name changed immediately and that she had to come up to the school tomorrow and announce at assembly that she made a mistake with my name and it was fixed now so they should stop calling me Fartboy.

Mum didn't seem to think that was a good idea, even after Jessica came in and said, 'Hello Fartboy, how are your farts today?'

I said to Mum, 'You can tell them my new name is Simon, okay? Like, Simon Matthew Augustus Reginald Tangles so that way I'm SMART.'

Mum said she didn't like the name Simon and that I was being silly. So I went and found the dictionary because the dictionary is never silly, and I looked up the word **fart**.

It said a fart was a release of intestinal gases through the anus, usually with an accompanying sound.

That didn't sound very silly to me. That sounded serious! Mum just laughed, saying how she always found farts funny and not very serious at all.

Fine then. I called her a fart. I called her *Fartmum*.

## 'How do you like that?'

It only made her laugh even more.

## It was so frustrating!

Mums don't understand anything!

So I went to the park.

Blocker, Tabby, Cooper and Scabs were already there. None of them mentioned anything about me being Fartboy at school. They were all feeling sorry for me.

I said to them all, 'Look on the bright side, at least my day can't get any worse.'

Just as I said it, Sid Malone and his gang rode into the park and came straight for us.

I never should have said it.

Suddenly being called Fartboy didn't matter at all. **Who cared?** Call me Fartboy all day long and I'll say yeah hi I'm Fartboy ... **anything!** If only Sid Malone wasn't riding straight for me. But he was, and the last thing he said to me before this was, **'I'll get you later, Freddy dead-ee.'**

He shouldn't have said that

We all looked at each other not knowing what to do.

Sid stopped right next to me and said, 'Whatta we got here then?'

None of us knew what to say, so we didn't say anything.

Sid pointed at Scabs's head where it was shaved and had stitches. He laughed really loud.

# 'HA! Good haircut!'

Tabby was about to do something stupid, like call Sid a name. I could tell because her lips had gone all tight, and she always did that when she was about to yell something. So I elbowed her and said to Sid, 'He's got stitches in his head from where a tree fell on him.'

'So?' Sid shot back. 'I've had stitches in me head too, hundreds of times, and it wasn't no stupid tree that did it. It was in a fight!'

We all looked at each other again.

Just saying the word **fight** seemed to make a fight really close to happening, and then it was like for sure when Sid's gang started whacking their fists into their hands.

Sid shoved me hard and barked,

# 'You got any money?'

I shook my head.

It wasn't the only
part of me that was
shaking, either. I was
shaking so much that
if coins were in my

pocket, they would have rattled.

I looked across at my friends. They were in trouble
too, except Tabby.

She was shouting at the gang guy near her, saying
how she had four older brothers and if he touched
her then he would get it and here, she had forty
cents and he could have it because he looked like
a homeless person who needed it!

She was amazing. The rest of us were stuck,
though, and I saw only one chance.

I had to unleash my power ...

If ever my laser-beam eyes were going to work, it
had to be right now ...

I latched my stare onto Sid and stared so hard
that my eyeballs actually started to hurt.

Sid picked me up by the front of my shirt.

### 'What are you lookin' at?'

That only worked to my advantage, because now my eyes were really close to his.

## 'STOP STARING LIKE THAT OR I'LL MAKE YOU STOP!'

I kept staring. Now was the time, with all hope lost and the hero about to get smashed ... this was the moment when my eyes would blast out laser beams!

I refused to even blink.

My eyes were watering bad, but I still didn't blink or look away because this **WOULD WORK ...**

## And I would save everyone!

Only nothing happened.

No way could laser beams work through all the water that was pouring out of my eyes.

I started blinking.

Before I knew it I was talking. I blurted out, 'Everyone at school called me Fartboy today.'

I don't know why I said it. I just had to say something, do something.

Sid put me down and said, 'Is that why you're crying, cry baby?'

His face was staring down at me and it was like the whole sky was filled with this fiery freckled snarling planet with big ears sticking straight out.

'I'm not crying,' I said. 'Just, just got something in my eye.'

'It'll be my fist in a minute,' Sid laughed.

If only I could run away. It was my only hope.

The problem was, even if I could have shaken free from Sid, my legs were too jelly to do anything.

Then he said, 'Fartboy, eh? Yeah, you do stink.'

His friends laughed. 'Yeah, you stink,' they kept saying.

At least they were laughing, which was better than punching. I had to keep talking.

'Yeah, this kid at school called me Fartboy, so I clobbered him.'

'Clobbered him, eh?' Sid liked that kind of talk.

'Yeah,' I blabbered. 'Then I bashed all his mates. And then ... and then I got in trouble with the principal!'

My words sounded so stupid to my ears, like the biggest, most obvious lie. I've never hit anyone. I wanted to stop talking but the words kept coming out.

Now he knows how we feel

Yeah!

'Stupid principal.'

Sid nodded like he knew a lot about principals.

'So they called you Fartboy, did they?'

'Yeah.'

'That school of yours is good at calling people names.'

That seemed like a weird thing for Sid to say, almost friendly. I asked, 'What do you mean?'

For a moment I thought he was going to tell me, but instead he snarled, **'Nothin'!'**

He pointed at my bike and I couldn't believe what he said.

'So you want to ride with us, Tangles?'

Ride? With SID?

He wanted me to ride in his gang!

There was no way I wanted to do that. I just wanted to get away, get home.

I said, 'Oh yeah, sure, oh but I can't, Mum won't let me. I'm late for home already.'

**'Your mum!'** laughed Sid. 'Who cares about your mum?'

'Yeah, not me.'

'Then let's go. Stuff your mum.'

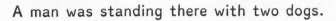

'Um ... okay.' I couldn't think of a way out.

'Oi, Malone!'

A man was standing there with two dogs.

'You leave those kids alone.'

Sid snarled at him, 'You can't tell me what to do, old man.'

'Maybe not, but my dog can.'

He had two dogs, a big brown muscly one and a little white fluffy one. I think he was talking about the big one because it was growling and you could see its teeth. The little one looked angry too, but more like an angry white tennis ball.

Sid left, saying all sorts of rude things. I breathed out the longest sigh of relief, and so did Blocker, Cooper and Scabs. Tabby just grumbled about bullies and who did they think they were?

Scabs said, 'I think your day's getting better now, Freddy.'

'Think you're right, Scabs.'

The dog that had saved my life was now wagging his tail and flopping out a friendly tongue so I put my hand out to pat him, only, I really wish I hadn't. The little white fluffball next to him jumped up and chomped onto my finger.

I couldn't believe it!

It bit down on my finger really hard. I tried to flick it off but it wouldn't let go.

I freaked. It was hanging onto my finger and I could feel its teeth digging in even deeper. I thought it might even bite my finger off!

# I started spinning.

I thought it might fly off but no, it just used my spinning like I was some crazy carnival ride for fluffy white dogs!

The man who owned the dog caught it as it flew past and tried to pull it off my finger.

But the little furball wouldn't let go until the man like, pulled open its jaws. Then he blamed me for upsetting his dog!

## No way was my day getting any better!

Of course Tabby had to ask, 'What would you rather be, a person bitten on the finger by a tiny dog, or a tiny dog stuck way up in the air like dangling over a cliff and only hanging on by your teeth?'

Even though no one said anything, it was obvious everyone was feeling more sorry for the dog than for me.

On the way home I asked Tabby how she managed to make the gang guy stay away from her.

'Oh, that. I have four older brothers, so I know how to stop them. I find their weakness and attack it. I know all my brothers' weaknesses, so they're all afraid of me.'

That was exactly what my sister was doing to me with my deep sleeping!

'And what was that gang guy's weakness?'

What's a finger for anyway?

Nothing! All anyone needs is legs and a mouth

'Easy. He's a coward. That's why he's in a gang. So I threatened him with my older brothers.'

When I got home I showed Mum my finger and she freaked.

I don't get it! She thought it was funny that I was called Fartboy by the entire school but then she freaks over a tiny dog bite. How does that work?

Mum said I might have to get a needle for the bite. A needle? A NEEDLE! No way was my day getting any better! She said I would have to go to the doctor tomorrow as it was too late today and that meant I couldn't go to school.

Hmmmm ... no school.

A needle or school?

If Tabby had given me that choice, normally the answer would have been school. Who wants a needle? But that wasn't the real question.

The real question was: a needle or getting called Fartboy? Maybe a needle wasn't so bad.

So at last, that was the end of my worst day ever.

The problem was, all the badness from my worst day ever overflowed into the next day.

Starting with the doctor!

Doctors are scary. Sid is scary too but different scary. I think the main difference is that doctors smile before they hurt you, while Sid smiles after he hurts you.

BEFORE

AFTER

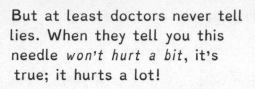

But at least doctors never tell lies. When they tell you this needle *won't hurt a bit*, it's true; it hurts a lot!

And that's not all they do. Once I had a splinter in my foot that was so big it nearly didn't fit in the car. It hurt so much that if someone even *looked* at the splinter it hurt even more!

So Mum took me straight to Doctor Malvoy who looked at my foot and smiled, so I knew what that meant, only he didn't just look at my foot to make it hurt more, he gave it a squeeze.

# A SQUEEZE!

Sid could never have hurt me as much as that squeeze did.

So I showed Doctor Malvoy my dog-bitten finger and he smiled ... before giving my finger a squeeze.

## WHY DOES HE ALWAYS SQUEEZE?

At least this time it didn't hurt so much as it was just a little dog bite so I was lucky. But I really think Doctor Malvoy should stop squeezing things.

Then he said, 'It looks quite clean, Mrs Tangles. Freddy is almost due for his vaccination shot so

I'll give it to him now. Better to be careful, don't you think?'

I thought, NO, but Mum nodded so needle it was.

'Okay, young man, drop your pants, this won't hurt a bit.'

There, he said it. Now I knew it was going to hurt a lot!

And I had to drop my pants. He was going to give me the needle in my bottom.

I don't know why Doctor Malvoy gives me some of my needles in my bottom. What's wrong with my arm? It's like some days he decides that he doesn't like bottoms and wants to stick needles in them.

And I think it's wrong!

I think bottoms get a really bad deal, like who would ever want to be one?

First of all, poo comes out of them, so that's pretty gross, not to mention farts and needles, and then they get sat on, whacked and kicked.

Most of the time it's not even their fault!

On top of all that, bottoms are really ugly, particularly my dad's. It is so hairy. My dad always makes the same joke: he comes into the room and pulls his pants down so we see his bum and he says, 'Oh no, I broke my bum! Look, it's got a big crack in it.'

Anyway, the doctor gave me the needle and it definitely hurt more than a bit, even though he said it wouldn't.

Mum bought me some ice cream after that. She was talking about sending me back to school for

the rest of the day so I pretended my bitten finger was hurting and my bum was hurting too. I started limping as well and even pretended the ice cream gave me a stomach-ache.

It worked! Mum let me stay home.

I spent most of the day thinking about one thing: getting called Fartboy at school.

The next morning I told Mum my finger was still really sore but she made me go to school.

She said, 'Don't worry about being called Fartboy. It's just a silly name and they will all forget very quickly.'

I asked her how fast quickly was because I remember dad once saying, 'This summer has gone by so quickly.' And like, I'm pretty sure summer lasted for three months!

I might try that, you know, pretend to be sick, get a day off.

You do know that if you show any sign of weakness, it is my duty to drag you back to the nest and feed you to the youngsters

Nothing wrong with me!

I also remember my great-granddad being nearly a hundred years old and saying his life seemed to have passed by so quickly.

# A hundred years!

So even saying they will forget very quickly doesn't mean I won't be called Fartboy for the next hundred years!

Mum said, 'I'm sure quickly won't be that long.'

I said, 'Oh yeah, well, how long is long?'

'What are you talking about?'

'Mum, no one knows how long long is.'

She just pushed me out the door saying, 'Everything will be fine,' but I wasn't so sure.

I remember Mr Brody once asked our class how long a piece of string was. Like, he didn't have the piece of string, he just wanted to know how long string was. No one put up their hand. It was a stupid question so I put up my hand and said, 'Well, sir, it depends on how long the string is.'

Which was a stupid answer because that was the question in the first place.

Mr Brody said, 'Exactly right, Freddy.'

I was a little bit proud of getting the answer right, even though I didn't have any clue at all what I was talking about or what Mr Brody was talking about either.

But, the thing is, nobody can say how long long actually is.

So anyway, I walked into school and passed some kids I knew and one of them looked up and said, 'Hi Freddy.'

# He called me Freddy!

It was like music to my ears. Quickly hadn't been very long at all. They had already forgotten about Fartboy.

# I was Freddy again!

I went down to the playground and Toby Mason called out, 'Hi Freddy.'

Yes!

Mum was right!

Then one kid yelled out, 'Hey, there's Fartboy!' He didn't say it mean or anything, it was like he just saw me and remembered and it burst out of his mouth.

'Oh yeah!' cried out Toby, who just a moment before had called me Freddy. 'Hi Fartboy,' he corrected. 'Freddy Fartboy.'

Before long it was through the playground and everyone thought it was funny all over again because jokes about farts are always funny.

So as it turned out, Mum was wrong. I did have something to worry about.

Kids were walking past holding their noses and whoofing at the air to get that farty smell to go away. Some pretended to run off as if a tiger or something really scary was chasing them. They were all having a great old time.

At least my friends didn't do anything like that. I sat among them with my head down so no-one could see me. It was nice to be hidden away.

Cooper came running in and said, kind of excited, 'You should see what Gilly and Matt are doing. They're making face masks out of paper and sticky tape and selling them so people won't be able to smell Fartboy. Like, heaps of people are lining up to buy them. We should make some too and sell them!'

Everyone was quiet and Cooper saw me for the first time.

'Oh ... but, it's not like you really do smell ... Just to make some money ...'

The rotting food we eat smells like farts

It's like we're eating farts

Tabby asked all of a sudden, 'What would you rather be, innocent of a crime but sent to jail for life anyway, or guilty of a crime and sent to jail for life?'

I wondered why Tabby was asking such a stupid question when I realised that she was talking about me, that I was innocent of being smelly.

But *life*?

Did she think I was going to be Fartboy for life?

Three kids walked past wearing the face masks. They looked right at me, waiting until I saw them, and when I did they laughed.

In class, everyone except my friends stayed as far away from me as they could get.

Mr Brody called me over and whispered, 'Sorry Freddy, I never would have let Scarlett mark the roll if I'd known this would happen.'

I told him it was okay and was about to go back to my chair when he said, 'You know, I once saw a seagull crash into a tree and break its wing.'

Well, I didn't know that. I started back to my seat again, only faster this time, when he started up again. 'You see, when one of us, you know, a human, is injured, we take them to the hospital to get fixed up, but not seagulls.'

I could have told him that, because I've never seen a seagull hospital.

Then he asked, 'Do you know what the other seagulls did when they saw that their friend had a broken wing?'

I shrugged and said, 'Took him back to his nest?'

'No, they attacked him. Here he was, injured and hurting, and the other gulls pecked him to death.'

'Oh,' I said, looking at my chair and wishing I was in it.

'Anyway, seeing the kids treat you so poorly, Freddy, reminds me of that seagull.'

'I'm not a seagull, sir,' I said, a little surprised he was talking about me.

'But the way they pick on you all together. It's terrible, terrible.'

Mr Brody shook his head and looked at me. 'You know, I think of that poor seagull quite often.'

I didn't know what to say, so I patted him on the shoulder and tried once again to get back to my chair, only to be stopped again!

He gave me a job to do. I had to go to every class to pass a note to the teachers about the gala day that was coming up. I think Mr Brody gave me the job to help me get away from my class for a while.

Only I wish he hadn't.

It was worse in the other classrooms. Every room I went in, the kids all whispered, 'There's Fartboy.'

I could hear them.

They all started lifting their feet off the ground so they wouldn't get my germs.

I know they were doing that because I used to do it to one girl. Her name was Penny Henderson.

It seemed like fun when I was doing it to her; we were all doing it together and it was like a big joke. I can't remember why we were doing it to Penny, something about her being dirty or something. We were lifting our feet off the ground so we didn't catch Penny Hendy Fever, and now they were lifting their feet so they didn't catch Freddy Fartboy Fever.

Now that it was happening to me, I realised just how mean we had been to Penny Henderson and if she was still at our school, I would tell her how sorry I was. But she left and I think I know why. I wanted to leave this school too and I didn't think anyone would care if I did. At least they wouldn't have to catch Freddy Fartboy Fever if I wasn't there.

It was like everyone together was saying,

Look at all those feet in the air

Don't go under them, it's a trap!

# GO AWAY!

## YOU SMELL AND WE DON'T WANT YOU HERE!

Maybe they didn't mean that, but that was what it felt like. They were being cruel and smiling their heads off at the same time.

Every room I went into was the same. I was starting to feel a bit like Mr Brody's seagull.

At lunch it didn't matter where I went. Kids would back away from me as if they might catch some deadly disease.

Scarlett Magnusson, who started it all in the first place, led pretend Fartboy tour parties through the school. I saw her stop in front of a patch of dead grass and say to them, 'This is where Fartboy first farted and killed all the grass.'

Then she pointed to a wall with some paint peeling off it and said, 'And you can see here how strong his farts are, they can even make paint fall off.'

She had like twenty kids following her around and they were all laughing. She even brought them over to my hang and said, 'And here we see Fartboy in his natural habitat, farting away and smelling really bad. And look, he's eating food to make more farts! Won't that be exciting ...'

Tabby told her to go away, which was really nice of her, but Scarlett just said, 'And these are

Fartboy's friends. They like to be near Fartboy because they like his smell.'

They all laughed again and one of them, Angus Pillick, walked up to me with one hand over his nose and poked me and said, 'Oh no, now I've got Freddy Fartboy Fever!'

We ants follow a smell trail all the time

Yeah, when we drop smells out of our bottoms everyone follows us

He touched someone else and yelled, 'Now you have it!'

That started a big game of chasings through the whole playground. Whoever was touched last had the fever.

Angus Pillick was a year older than me so I didn't really know him very well. He came over again and said he needed some more of my fever to secretly infect a teacher.

I wasn't really sure what to do because he was bigger than me, and his friends were there too, so I just sat there.

Blocker and Cooper stood up.

Blocker told him to go away but Angus said, 'Make me.'

They just sort of stood in front of each other until Angus tried to push past, but Blocker pushed him back.

Some kids started yelling, **'Fight!'**

I jumped up. I don't know what I was thinking but I ran past Block and jumped on Angus. We fell to the ground. I had my arms around him in a big bear hug and was holding on as hard as I could.

He couldn't get free, and I was yelling,

## 'Now you've got the fever all over you! You can't ever get rid of it. Ever. Ever!'

Someone pulled me off him and someone else kicked me, or maybe a few people did, because it was crazy. There were kids everywhere. Angus punched me in the stomach and that hurt and then Mr Brody pulled me up and I was dangling in the air.

# 'Settle down, boys!'

'He started it!' Angus yelled. 'He jumped on me!'

'Is that true, Freddy?'

That's not a fight

Yeah, they're not even biting each other!

I was almost breathless as I blurted out, **'He wanted Fartboy Fever, so I gave it to him!'**

I think I saw Mr Brody smile a little bit when he said quietly, 'So the seagull fights back.'

Then he raised his voice for everyone to hear.

'Right. You're all on notice. If I hear of anyone teasing Freddy anymore they will be on detention for a week. And just so it's clear, Freddy doesn't smell any different to anyone else. Understood?'

Everyone was quiet.

## 'Well, is it?'

He was looking straight at Angus, who eventually said, 'Yes sir.'

It was really nice of Mr Brody to say that, but as soon as he was gone it didn't make any difference.

When I passed by kids in the hall they squeezed over to the far side to get past. If I met someone in a doorway they backed away as if I was holding a gun or something.

When school was over I was so relieved, until I saw that Angus was waiting for me.

He watched me walk away from school, out of the teachers' sight, before running up.

'You're done for, Fartboy,' he said, and pushed me backwards.

I suddenly felt really angry, like,

# WOULD THIS NEVER END?

In my experience, a fight is only ever over when you bite their head off

Or rip their legs off

Angus pushed me again, hard, and I fell over. He kicked my leg. 'Get up, come on, get up.'

I got up and he came at me again. I stuck out my hands like I was going to box him even though I didn't know how.

Angus backed away and suddenly went pale. I thought for a moment it must have been my boxing hands but it wasn't, it was ... my little sister!

Jessica came barrelling past me and told Angus to go away. It seemed weird that he was so afraid of my little sister, he doesn't even sleep in the same room as her.

But then it all made sense when he kept looking behind me and not at Jessica at all.

'What have we got here then?'

It was a sound that sent chills of fear down my spine: the voice of Sid!

'I'm the only one around here that does the bashing,' he said.

Great, I thought. Getting bashed by Angus Pillick was bad enough, but Sid Malone!

Angus called out nervously, 'Just finishing something he started, Sid.'

Which I think was totally unfair. I started it because they called me Fartboy and he wanted to poke me AND he followed me after school.

'He started it, eh?' Sid moved closer. 'I heard he was a fighter.'

He'd heard that because I told him, but that was all lies.

Sid grabbed my shirt in a fist and lifted me off the ground. I was dangling in front of him.

He growled into my face, 'You might have started the fight but I'm gonna finish it.'

That was it, my life was over.

Sid went on, 'Nobody beats up a member of my gang.'

I didn't even know that Angus was a member of his gang!

He let go of me and went over to Angus. 'You've picked on a member of my gang, which means you've picked on me.'

Angus looked from Sid to me in shock.

'I didn't know!' he cried. 'You didn't tell me!' he wailed at me. 'Sid, he never told me!'

'Then I'll tell you.'

Sid pushed him over as easy as a piece of cardboard.

'Now you've been told.'

I was struggling to keep up. First I was going to get beaten up by Angus, then it was Sid and now Sid was fighting for me! I needed Blocker to put his finger in my mouth right now because it was open wide enough for ten flies to get in.

Sid's gang came up and stood around me. Angus scrambled back to his feet and ran away.

# 'Run away!'

I yelled.

# 'CHICKEN!'

# 'Malone!'

It was Mr Brody. He
told Sid to go away but
Sid didn't. He said it was a public street and he
didn't have to do what a teacher told him to do.

Mr Brody grabbed me and took me back into the
school.

**'See ya! Thanks!'** I yelled back at Sid and he
nodded darkly.

Mr Brody pulled me into the school office. 'What
do you think you're doing with that boy, Tangles?'

'He saved me from Angus, sir. Angus followed
me out of school and wanted to fight me but Sid
stopped him.'

Mr Brody gave a sharp nod. 'Right, I'll deal
with Mr Pillick tomorrow. As for Sid, he is nothing
but trouble and you have to stay away from him.'

'Okay,' I said, a bit confused because Sid did just
save me. 'But maybe he's getting better, sir.'

Mr Brody let out a noise like what I said was too
stupid for words. 'Did he want you in his gang?'

'Um, yeah, he sort of got Angus because I was in his gang.'

## 'You're in his gang?!'

'No! No way! He asked me but I never said I wanted to.'

'Good! Whatever you do, Freddy, don't join.'

'I wouldn't, sir.'

'Good boy.' Mr Brody seemed pleased.

'Sir, do you know why Sid is so mean?'

Mr Brody looked at me for a good long second, as if wondering whether he should say anything, and then he did.

'Sid's a troubled kid, Freddy. His family is ... well, he never had much of a chance, I'm afraid. I sometimes wish I'd tried harder for him when he was a student here.'

'Were you his teacher, sir?'

'For a while I was.'

'What was he like?'

Mr Brody gave me another one of those wondering looks.

'I'll tell you this about him, Freddy. When Sid was here, he used to get teased, a little like you're getting teased now.'

'Really? What did he get teased about?'

'You don't remember?'

I shook my head.

'I suppose it was some years ago. Well, he wasn't very good at school and ... tell me, Freddy, when you look at Sid, what do you see?'

'Um, a big scary guy.'

'And?'

'Well ... he does have big ears that stick straight out.'

'Not very bright and with big ears. What do you think the kids called him?'

I shrugged. 'Sid?' He was too big to call a name no matter what he looked like.

'No, they called him Dumbo, you know, after the baby elephant in the Disney movie who had big ears.'

So that's what Sid meant when he said, 'That school is good at calling people names.'

He was just like me!

DUMBO!

'So he was a seagull too.'

Mr Brody was about to nod then stopped himself. 'No! You are not like Sid. You might be getting teased but that will pass.'

I dropped my eyes. 'I don't think so, sir. It's my name now and there's nothing anyone can do to stop it.'

Dumbo, Fartboy ... Sid and I had a big thing in common.

I had to sit in the school office for another ten minutes before Mr Brody would let me out. My friends and my sister were still waiting for me.

We talked about Angus and Sid all the way home. No one could believe that Sid had come to my rescue; it just seemed too impossible.

I wasn't sure if I should tell Mum about what happened, but I had no choice because Jessica blurted it out the moment we went inside.

Well your antennas are stupid

Oh ... that's very hurtful

And you have a butt face

Stop that!

Mum made me promise I would never join Sid's gang and I was fine about that. No way did I want to join Sid's gang. To be in a gang that went around hurting people was just wrong.

The next day at school I was Fartboy again. Nothing had changed. As far as everyone at school was concerned, I was Fartboy yesterday and I was Fartboy today.

Scarlett was still enjoying her fame as the finder of Fartboy. She explained to her followers how the leaves on the ground fell off the tree because of my farts and the crack in the concrete where we sat was from what she called the Great Fart of February, which happened after I ate too many beans.

I told her to go away but she only said, '**Look out! He'll fart on us if we stay here ... RUN!**'

They ran off as if they were running for their lives.

Angus went past and when he saw me he put his head down and didn't hold his nose at all. He was about the only kid in the entire school who wasn't pretending that I smelt. He had a good reason not to ... he was afraid of Sid.

Afraid of Sid ... hmmm ... that gave me an idea.

I went over to Angus and told him that Sid wanted him to tell everyone in the school that I was in Sid's gang, and if they didn't stop teasing me, Sid would get them.

Angus said he wouldn't do it so I told him that Sid would be waiting for him after school.

Well, that changed everything. He went around from group to group and he even got his friends to help him do it.

He told everyone that I was in Sid's gang. By recess I was definitely getting teased less.

Mr Brody needed another message sent around to the classes about the gala day so I volunteered. In just about every room I went into, kids were still lifting their feet to avoid catching the fever. I said in a loud voice,

**'Put your feet down or you know what will happen!'**

# And they did!

There's nothing like having a Sid on your side to make people do what you want them to.

The rest of the day was so cool.

If anyone so much as held their nose I wrote their name down on a piece of paper.

This was the piece of paper ...

When they found out that their name was on the list, they came over and apologised and asked if their name could be taken off it.

My friends thought my plan was awesome.

Blocker even said, 'You have defeated my saying, you have stopped the river of words.'

'Thanks to the power of Sid!' I cried.

'Yeah. Great idea,' said Blocker, shaking his head in admiration at my genius.

Tabby disagreed. She said that I shouldn't be on Sid's side even if it was pretend, and to remember all the bad things he'd done.

I remembered alright. I said that using Sid's name was payment for all the bad things he'd done, that at last he was doing something good, even if it was just lending me his name.

She said, 'How can you call this good? You're threatening people with Sid! By doing this you're becoming like him.'

'No I'm not! All I'm doing is stopping people from teasing me.'

She said, 'You're playing with fire, Freddy, and if you play with fire, you **will** get burnt.'

I said, 'I'm sorry, Tabby, but Block is in charge of sayings.'

She just huffed.

Everything was going great until Mr Brody found out about my list of kids to be bashed by Sid.

Scarlett Magnusson was crying in class because she was the last one on the list and I wouldn't take her name off it. Why would I? She started it all and she really rubbed my nose in it. Anyway,

before long Mr Brody had my list in his hand. He tore it up and threw it in the bin.

He told me enough was enough and he was right. I never intended to give the list to Sid anyway, or hopefully, to ever see him again.

And anyway, it had worked. Everyone had stopped calling me Fartboy.

It was all over ...

I was so happy. When I got home I told Mum how no one was calling me Fartboy anymore and she said, 'See, I told you they would forget quickly.'

I didn't tell her about the list and how I pretended to be in Sid's gang. I was too afraid to do that. She would have been mad at me for sure.

When she asked me how it happened I just said, 'Oh, they realised it was mean and so they stopped.'

'That's great, they must really like you to listen to you like that.'

That wasn't the reason. I felt a bit guilty about not telling her. A lot guilty, actually. I left for the park. After a little while, Tabby and Blocker turned up.

Tabby asked, 'So what did your mum think about your Sid list?'

Tabby really knew where to dig for weaknesses. No wonder her brothers were afraid of her.

'She thought it was a good idea.'

Blocker nodded. 'It was a great idea!'

'Yeah!' We high-fived.

Tabby kept staring at me. 'You didn't tell her, did you? You were afraid of what she would say.'

'You're just jealous about how good I am at playing with fire.'

Sid and his gang rode into the park. He rode right up to me and said, 'So let's go.'

'Me? Go where?'

'Ridin'.'

'Like in your gang?'

'We heard you been telling everyone you're in our gang. So let's see how you go.'

They'd heard!

I didn't know what to do.

'Come on. Hurry up.'

I looked at Tabby and Blocker and I could see they were scared and I was too. I asked them if they wanted to ride as well but they didn't.

Tabby said, 'I don't hang around with losers.'

Block just shook his head. Sid's gang was staring at me, waiting. My only choices right now were to ride or run.

Tabby said, 'The best thing for a burn is to run it under cold water.'

I think she was giving me a hint that I should run. But they were all right there and ... I was too afraid to run ...

'Okay,' I said.

How bad could it be anyway?

The three gang guys with Sid came over and high-fived me.

Their names were Jimmy, Vinnie and Toddo.

We rode out of the park.

Blocker and Tabby watched me go and I saw Tabby shake her head and mouth the word 'run'.

Sid rode up next to me.

'So they still calling you that name?'

'No. I told them not to and they stopped.'

'Yeah, that school, I made them pay for calling me a name too. You belong with us.'

It was so strange riding with Sid. Every time we went past kids they moved away or hid, like I used to. Vinnie was riding next to me and he said to me, 'See, they're all chickens and we can do anything we like because we've got the respect!'

'So do you guys ever kick the footy around?' I asked, seeing as it was one my most favourite things to do.

Vinnie looked at me like I was some kind of alien.

'Footy?'

'You know, when you're not riding, scaring ... er, getting respect.'

'No. We ride until something happens.'

Something happened.

Toddo flattened someone's letterbox!

He ran it over on his bike and then stomped on it until it was flat. Jimmy, Vinnie and Sid laughed and told Toddo to stomp more. I started laughing too. I mean, I didn't like what he was doing and I so wished he would stop, but I still laughed because I had to. They were watching me to see if I did.

'See,' said Vinnie, 'we do what we like.'

I didn't like it.

Vinnie handed me a football that some kids left behind when they ran away from us.

'Here you go, you want to kick a footy, kick this away.'

They all watched me.

'Kick it where?'

'Away! Where they won't find it.'

I kicked it as hard as I could. It went right over a house.

Sid approved. 'Lucky to find that again.'

I watched the ball fly away and wished that it was me.

We rode off until Sid stopped next to three kids playing by the street. He got off his bike and grabbed one of them by the shirt. He lifted him right off the ground, growled at him like he was a dog and then dropped him.

The kid kind of crumpled at Sid's feet.

Sid said to me, 'Freddy, fight him.'

And I'm like, what? Fight him? I didn't want to fight him. I didn't even know him.

Sid said, 'Fight him now or you're not in our gang, and if you're not in our gang then you're one of them.'

When he said 'them' he pointed to the kid on the ground.

Vinnie, Jimmy and Toddo were nodding too. I looked over at them, trying to work out what was going on. They were nodding for me to do it but it was

These humans seem to enjoy their work

Enforcing your territory is good gang work

more than just for fun, it looked like they really wanted me to do it, needed me to do it. They were pleading with their eyes for me to do it.

'But what for?' I asked Sid.

# 'Because I said so!'

He looked so fierce.

I realised that this was my initiation and that if I didn't fight the kid then Sid and his gang would bash me.

I looked back at the others and they were still nodding. But there was something about the way they were looking at me that I couldn't work out, as if they were frightened for me ...

That didn't matter though. What mattered was Sid. He was yelling, **'Come on, Freddy,'** and thumping my shoulder, pushing me towards the kid.

The kid was about my size. He was standing up again, eyes wide and scared. His two friends were stuck with Vinnie and Jimmy and Toddo.

I didn't do anything so Sid yelled, **'FIGHT HIM!'** right in my ear and shoved me so that I bumped into the kid.

## 'Fight him to prove you're one of us.'

I put my hands into fists.

They were all yelling at me to punch the kid, who had started crying. There was so much noise and shoving. Somehow through all the confusion

I thought of Tabby and how she had called this gang cowards.

I was a coward too. I couldn't stand up to Sid. I couldn't even run away when I had the chance. I couldn't even tell my mum the truth. All because I was afraid. Maybe I deserved to be here. Maybe this was where all cowards who get called names in school end up.

I got shoved into the kid again, and I pushed him hard.

'Yeah, Freddy,' called Sid. **'PUNCH HIM!'**

I was thinking that maybe I could punch the kid if he punched me first.

'Come on, punch me,' I said to him, almost begging him.

The kid just sobbed, 'I ... I ... I'm sorry.'

'What for? For being so stupid?' I said, hoping it would make him punch me.

He said, 'For whatever I did wrong.'

The thing was, he hadn't done anything wrong.

# HE HADN'T DONE ANYTHING WRONG!

I was the one doing wrong.

It was me and I knew it and I knew that I couldn't fight him.

I wasn't a bully.

I hated what Sid and his gang were.

# I HATED IT!

There was no way I was going to be like them. I had a choice and I was going to make it.

So I turned back to Sid.

Sid was looking extra big and mean and he was shouting at me,

'Come on, Freddy, knock his block off.'

Vinnie, Toddo and Jimmy were also yelling at me.

I shouted back, 'NO!'

Sid shut his mouth, stunned.

He was even more stunned by what I said next. I pointed at the kid and then his friends.

## 'Not just him ... I want to knock all their blocks off!'

Sid's face broke into the most massivest evilest grin you ever saw.

'All three of them? You want to smash all three of them? Yeah, smash 'em all!'

Vinnie, Jimmy and Toddo pushed the other two kids towards me and then circled around so they couldn't run away.

I grabbed the kid in front of me and put him in a headlock. He was still crying. I could tell that he was super scared.

While I had him in the hold I whispered in his ear ...

'When I say run, you follow me as fast as you can and tell your friends to follow too.'

'Okay,' he whispered back.

I pushed him away and threw a punch that missed him and yelled,

## 'NEXT TIME THAT PUNCH IS GONNA SMASH YOUR FACE!'

Sid and the others were calling for me to do it, so I stood there with my hands on my hips and said, 'I'll give you three a chance. Go on, huddle together, come up with a battle plan, and then I'll smash you all.'

Sid was really impressed.

## 'You rock, Freddy!'

They huddled together and I knew that they were talking about what I had whispered.

After a while I yelled, **'Time's up!'**

They broke up all nervous, and I started saying, **'Chickens, look at the chickens. Chickens!'**

Sid and the others were yelling as well. They were all around us in a circle and it was so noisy.

They were yelling **fight, fight,** and pushing the kids closer to me.

Meanwhile, I was looking to see where my bike was and where they needed to run to get away and so I was moving around, and when we were in the right position I yelled,

# 'RUN!!!'

And ran straight at Jimmy.

He wasn't expecting anything like that.

I crashed straight into him, bowled him over and the three kids charged through the hole I made and bolted off.

As it turned out, it didn't matter where they ran because Sid and his gang were only interested in catching one person, and that was me.

# 'AFTER HIM!'

I had a head start but Toddo caught up to me in no time at all and grabbed my shoulder.

Sid yelled, 'Rip him off his bike!'

I felt Toddo's grip tighten so I swerved away, making Toddo veer straight into a gutter.

'Get him!' yelled Sid. 'Don't let him go!'

One of their wheels nudged my back mudguard and I nearly went down. Jimmy swung an arm at my head and I ducked. He slammed his bike into the side of mine and I would have gone down for sure, but I jumped my bike over the gutter and onto the footpath.

'Get him! We're gonna pulverise you!'

Vinnie flew over the gutter after me, but just as he went to grab me I jumped the gutter back onto the road — right into the path of Sid, who swung his arm to knock me off, but I veered away and there it was in the distance ... HOME!

I had to move fast. They were boxing me in but I thought I could make it ... until one of them threw a stick in my back wheel. My bike bucked like bull and shot off sideways straight into Toddo, knocking him over. They had me trapped! They all wheeled around between me and my house like an impossible wall across the road.

Sid got off his bike. 'We've got you now, Tangles, and you're gonna pay!'

A car on the road behind me honked its horn. The wall of bikes gave way to the car. This was my chance! As the car went past, I tucked in behind it, straight past Sid!

I heard swearing as I charged up my driveway and into the garage. I leapt off my bike and ran into the house, leaving the bike to rattle across the garage floor.

Sid yelled so loud that the whole neighbourhood must have heard ...

I was so scared. I couldn't see anyone in the house so I hid in a wardrobe. I was sure Sid would come in and get me.

I sat puffing in the darkness of the wardrobe listening desperately for the sound of Sid coming into the house, but there was only the sound of me trying to get my breath back.

Slowly, everything I had done came crashing in. I had been so stupid!

I thought of Block and how he would have never joined that gang, of Cooper who was too cool and Scabs who was too nice and Tabby ... who was too smart ... 'run', she had whispered and I hadn't because I wasn't brave enough ... until it was too late, until I made Sid my enemy.

I joined his gang and then I left. Nothing could be worse. Sid was going to hunt me down.

Mum came home and everything came out. I told her about pretending to be in Sid's gang to stop people calling me Fartboy and joining his gang and running away because it was so terrible and now how Sid Malone was after me.

'Why did you ever pretend to be in Sid's gang?' asked Mum.

'They were calling me Fartboy.'

'But it was just a silly name!'

'It isn't! Not to me. The whole school was calling me that and it hurt and I had a way of stopping it so I did. I'm sorry, sorry I did it and sorry I joined Sid's gang but I was just so scared and now everything is worse!'

'Well, I'm sorry I didn't take the name-calling more seriously. I'm sure we can fix this.'

That was easier said than done.

Every day Sid stopped outside my house and called out ...

It was so scary.

Mum would run out onto the street every time
Sid called but he just rode slowly away.

One of our windows got smashed with a rock
and one day our letterbox disappeared. It had to
be Sid but no-one saw him do it.

Mum wouldn't let me go anywhere on my own. She
dropped me off at school and picked me up, and
when I wasn't at school I had to stay at home.

Not even Dad could stop him.

He found out where Sid lived and went over to
talk to his parents but that didn't work. Dad
found out that Sid's parents were worse than Sid.

Sid's dad told my dad that if he didn't go away,
then he would belt him. He sounded just like Sid!
Which did make me feel a bit sorry for
Sid. He was teased at school and
when he went home he had bullies
for parents.

That would be really tough.

Sid came past my house every
day for two weeks. After
that he started coming
over less but it didn't seem
to matter. You just didn't
know when he would
appear. It was so freaky.

The one thing I was allowed to do was run over to Block's house because he lives just across the street. But even that was scary. It felt like Sid was hiding behind every tree or car.

It was while I was sneaking over to Blocker's house one day I that came up with a plan. The answer was so easy!

As soon as I saw Block I told him, 'Block, we need to move to Russia.'

No way could Sid get me if I was in Russia.

Block didn't seem all that keen but I was like, 'Yeah, come on, let's go, it's a perfect plan.' I told him we could live together in the same house. We could be like Russian brothers and I could change my name so Sid would never find me.

I asked him what Russian name I should have and he said I looked like a cousin of his called Bogdan.

Bogdan?

I never knew that I looked like a Bogdan. Still, anything was better than Freddy Fartboy and getting beaten up by Sid, so Bogdan it was.

Block said it didn't matter what I called myself. He wasn't going back to Russia, no matter what.

Okay, fine ... then maybe I could stay with some of his relatives ... maybe with Bogdan.

That was it!

I was moving to Russia to live with Bogdan and be called Bogdan.

It's funny how things change. A couple of minutes ago I was doomed to be bashed by Sid, but now I was going to live in Russia for the rest of my life and be called Bogdan.

BOGDAN

Block's mum came in and gave us some cookies and I said, 'Thank you, Mrs Dukarsky,' because I know how much she likes good manners. 'And thank you for letting me stay with your relatives in Russia.'

She said, 'Freddy, you have been a good friend to my Ivan, the best friend he has ever had, so I will help you.'

I said, 'Thank you, Mrs Dukarsky, but you can call me Bogdan from now on. Do you know where in Russia I will live?'

'No, you will not be going to Russia,' she said. 'And you will not be changing your name. You will stay here and you will stand up to this boy. You will be the Russian bear. We have a saying in Russia ...'

Actually, they seem to have a lot of sayings in Russia.

Mrs Dukarsky said, 'If the Tsar will not help us, there is no Tsar.'

I didn't have the first clue what she was talking about. I knew that Tsar was their word for king and that he liked to wear clothes, but that was it. She had to explain the rest.

'It means, if there is no one to help you, Freddy, then you must help yourself. You cannot be the mushroom any longer.'

I thought I was the Russian bear. Now I'm a mushroom?

Then she said, 'You must walk out and meet this boy.'

Okay, now I knew she was **crazy.**

So I said, 'Thanks, Mrs Dukarsky, but I need to go home now.'

I started to leave but she gripped my shoulders really hard and stared right into my eyes.

'Listen to me, Freddy Tangles. Nothing that this bully can do to you is worse than the fear he has gripped you with right now.'

Maybe that was true. I was scared all the time. And that included right now with the staring of Mrs Dukarsky.

She said, 'In Russia we fight. Sometimes we die but we have a saying ...'

Oh no, another one.

'The hammer shatters glass but it also forges steel.'

I really wanted to get away from her now. I couldn't take any more sayings.

'I have a hammer at home,' I suggested. 'I'll go and get it for you.'

I tried to leave but she wouldn't let me go.

'No Freddy, it is time for you to be the steel.'

'I'll just go home and ask my mum.'

Mrs Dukarsky stamped her foot really hard. 'No! When the eagle is flying, he doesn't need his mother to count his wing beats.'

I'm pretty sure that was another saying.

'Go out and meet this boy, Freddy. Your fears will end only when you do this.'

I wished she would stop telling me to go out and meet Sid because

# No WAY was I doing that!

It was just too stupid. Like, no-one ever goes and shakes a beehive just so the bees can come out and sting them or like, no-one goes into the ocean and calls, 'Here, sharky-sharky, dinner time!'

People don't do that and they don't go outside to get bashed by Sid.

Or go up to an anteater and ask what that long stupid tongue's for

Definitely don't do that

It was just crazy and I was so relieved when Blocker pulled me away from his mum.

Blocker knew what it meant to face Sid.

But then he said, 'I'll come with you.'

I was a bit confused at first. For a moment I thought he was saying that he was going to come with me to meet Sid like his crazy mum wanted me to. But then I realised he must mean that he was coming to Russia with me after all.

That was really good news. At least it was until he said, 'We'll meet Sid together.'

## Like, WHAT?

And his mum said, 'Of course you will, Ivan, you are his friend. You will go with Freddy to meet this Sid boy.'

Surely Block was joking, or maybe he was just pretending so that I could escape his mum? That must be it ... yes ... but no, he was nodding his head and agreeing with her, saying, 'That's what friends do.'

## He was AGREEING!

I couldn't believe what I was hearing.

Blocker wanted to come with me, to get beaten up by Sid, and his mum was going to let him! In fact, she thought it was a good idea!

I just looked at the two crazy Russians, smiling back at me, being as brave as anything ... and it hit me.

I was actually going to do it.

I was going to go outside and stand up to Sid.

# I was actually going to do it!

I was going to be crazy too.

No, not crazy ... I was going to be the Russian bear, and oh yeah, I was also going to be steel for when I got hammered by Sid, and I was going to flap my wings like an eagle too ...

I was going to face up to Sid.

I had never felt more brave in my entire life.

Or more scared.

'Okay,' I said.

It was such a little word, okay, but it meant so much. My heart was thumping in my chest like a hammer.

'Alright then,' said Mrs Dukarsky, clapping her hands. She opened the front door and stepped aside.

'You mean like **now?**'

'Why not?'

Why not? Like for starters I hadn't even written a will. Who was I going to leave all my stuff to after I was dead?

And what about Mum? I hadn't properly thanked her for all the dinners or Dad for teaching me how to ride a bike or Jessica for ... for ... I'm sure if I had more time I could have thought of something!

I thought it was important that I did things like that before Sid killed me.

'Well,' I said. 'Maybe we can do it after my birthday.'

I was pretty sure Dad was buying me a fishing rod so maybe after I caught some fish with that, and oh yeah, then there was Christmas too.

Mrs Dukarsky stamped her foot hard.

'**No! You do it now!** You face up to this boy, and you be brave, like the bear!'

I just stood there. I didn't know what to do or say. My legs wouldn't work. There was no way I could walk through that door even if I wanted to.

Blocker said, 'Come on, Freddy, we can do this together. We'll show Sid something he'll never forget.'

And I was thinking ... Yeah, like how to bleed to death.

Block said, 'We'll get everyone together. We'll have so many people by the time he finds us, that we'll beat him.'

It never occurred to me that we could actually win a fight against Sid but what Block said made sense. A lot of kids had a grudge against him. We could have a gang of our own.

Blocker went to the door and kissed his mother goodbye. She started tucking in his shirt like she always did, until he stopped her.

'No, Mother, this is not a time for manners.'

NOT BUSINESS     BUSINESS

His mum nodded and Block pulled his shirt back out. Now I knew that he really meant business.

There was nothing left to do except go. Blocker touched my shoulder and together we walked out of the house.

Before I knew it we were walking down the street. I felt kind of light-headed, like I was in a dream. Or maybe my brain just couldn't believe it was floating down the street inside a head that had decided to get smashed.

*where did you say I was going?*

I was definitely starting to feel scared again.

'We can beat Sid,' said Blocker, noticing how scared I looked. 'If we have enough people with us, we can actually beat him.'

We walked towards the park. We called up to Cooper's house as we passed and he came out with Scabs. Further up the road we saw the boy I saved from Sid, and his friends. His name was Ben and he said they'd been trying to find me to thank me.

I told them I was going to find Sid right now and fight him.

Ben said, 'You saved us so we'll help you fight him.'

Suddenly there were seven of us. We really could win!

We passed more kids and some of them joined us and others didn't. Everyone who joined us said they were sick of Sid and wanted to help. Soon there were thirteen of us!

Then we were fourteen because Tabby came up the street.

'I called her,' said Cooper.

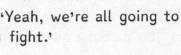

She came straight up to me. 'You're really going to fight Sid?'

'Yeah, we're all going to fight.'

She looked at us all.

## 'Are you crazy?'

I said, 'No, I'm a Russian bear.'

Blocker nodded, which was helpful, as Tabby was looking at me as if maybe my brains had already been rattled.

'A Russian bear?'

I could see that she was struggling with the Russian bear thing. Maybe I shouldn't have mentioned it.

## 'So you are crazy then!'

I tried to explain. 'No, I'm a Russian bear who is made of steel for when the hammering starts.'

'Like a hammering from Sid?'

'Yeah ... I mean no, we can beat him if we fight all together, can't we, guys?'

They all called out, **'Yes!'**

Blocker said, 'We can be a gang too. A better one than his gang.'

'A gang?' Tabby was starting to scrunch her mouth. 'You know that Sid and his gang will fight all of you as hard as anything. A lot of you will get hurt.'

'We're ready for anything!'

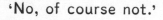

Tabby grabbed my arm. **'You come over here right now!'**

She pulled me away from the others.

Cooper called out, 'Ooooh, looks like Freddy's in trouble with his girlfriend.'

Tabby ignored him.

'A lot of you are going to get hurt. Is that what you want?'

Sounds like fun!

Can't wait!

'No, of course not.'

'So you've started a gang!'

'No we haven't. It's just for this, to get Sid.'

'You're doing what Sid would do!'

'No I'm not!'

'Yes you are! A gang to beat up people.'

'Well, how else do we beat him? He's too strong.'

'So you're going to let your friends get hurt.'

I looked over at my friends. I didn't know what to do.

'What choice do I have?'

'You're the Russian bear. They don't fight in packs. A Russian bear fights his own battles.'

'So you want me to fight Sid on my own?' That was madness. 'I'm not that stupid, or brave!'

'Who says you're not brave? I think you are.'

'But you know I'm not. You saw me when I joined Sid's gang. I was too scared to even run away.'

'But you did in the end. When you realised how bad it was, you ran away and you saved some kids doing it.'

Those kids were standing just a little way from me right now. They were there because I saved them, and now what was I getting them into?

Tabby went on, 'I think those kids would say that you were brave.'

She didn't know they were standing there, ready to fight for me.

'But I was still running away. I wasn't standing and fighting. There's no way I can fight Sid, so just forget it! I'm not doing it!'

'I don't want you to fight either.'

# 'Then what do you want?!'

'I have four older brothers that I stand up to, and you know how I do that?'

'Yeah,' I said impatiently. I felt like going back to my friends. Tabby wasn't helping. 'You know their weaknesses. You told me that.'

'And it works. So what's Sid's weakness?'

I breathed in deep, resisting the urge to walk away. 'I don't know ... he's over-confident, um, and there's only four of them and a lot more of us ...'

'No! That's fighting stuff. What did you notice when you were with them, as a gang?'

I had thought of my ride with the gang a million times in the last three weeks, wondering how I could have done it differently.

Tabby added, 'Maybe how they talked ... were there any who didn't like each other ...'

Suddenly it hit me. Of course!

Of course it's fighting talk, it's fight time!

I can't believe he's listening to her

'Tab, I think I know.'

'Great! What is it?'

'They ... it's the gang ... they ... I ...'

I think I knew what to do.

'Let me think about it while we walk.'

'Okay, but just remember, you can't win by fighting. Even if you won the fight today, they would be back tomorrow. Don't fight, no matter how much you want to.'

'I won't. I don't think I need to.'

I went back to the others.

'So what did your girlfriend tell you to do?' asked Cooper.

'She's not my girlfriend!'

I've never had a girlfriend and wouldn't have the slightest clue how to have a girlfriend, but if I ever did have one ...

I looked back at Tabby and silently mouthed, 'Thanks, Tab.'

I knew what I had to do. I just wondered if I was brave enough to do it.

We continued along the road towards the park.
Our numbers grew. Scabs counted eighteen!

Sid came into view. He turned his bike in our
direction, and so did Vinnie, Toddo and Jimmy.

They stopped in front of us and started laughing.

'**So** the **chicken** has come out of his chook
house and brought all the other chickens with him.'

Sid came closer.
He towered over me.

I said, 'I'm not
afraid of you
anymore, Sid.'

He leaned forward
really quickly and
whispered, 'Boo,'
super softly.

I count
eighteen little
ones against
four big ones

It's like eighteen of
us taking on a patrol
of those soldier ants

Gonna
be a great
fight

I jumped back in shock.

He laughed. 'Oh yeah? I think you might be a little scared, Tangles.'

He looked at the lot of us. 'So you got your own gang now, eh? Looks pretty puny. Is that your gang's name, the **Punies?**'

Sid's gang laughed at that and called out,

# 'PUNIES, look at the PUNIES!'

Blocker was right by my side and he growled, 'Let's get them, they can't beat us all.'

Blocker was ready for a fight.

I shook my head and said quietly, 'No fighting.'

Block exploded, **'WHY NOT?** Our gang might be puny but there's eighteen of us!'

'No, Block. We can't win by fighting, and we're not a gang.'

I knew Tabby was right. If only I could be brave enough.

I called to Sid, 'This isn't my gang, Sid. These are my friends and they aren't

Ever been in a gang fight?

Yeah, me and about 500 others attacked a nest last week

Who won?

No idea

afraid of me like Vinnie and Toddo and Jimmy
are afraid of you.'

Vinnie, Toddo and Jimmy laughed at that.

They were mucking around, but I knew what it was
like to be in Sid's gang. I also remembered the look
they gave me when Sid was forcing me to fight.

They were afraid of him.

I said to Sid, 'They follow you because they're
afraid of you. That's why I followed you too. But
us here, we're just friends. My friends don't have
to be here if they don't want to.'

I looked over at his gang. 'Vinnie, Jimmy, Toddo,
you don't need to follow him anymore. You can
just walk away and you'll be okay. You can be
friends with us.'

The three of them looked at each other.

Vinnie said, 'What's he talking about?'

Jimmy called to me, 'You got your facts wrong.
We ain't going anywhere.'

Sid laughed, 'Brilliant!
Was that your brilliant
plan for today, Tangles?'

'No.'

It actually was. Most of it.

I said, 'We're also here to say how sorry we all feel for you.'

'Sorry for me!' laughed Sid. 'You're the one who's about to get belted, you and all your puny friends.'

Nothing was working. I knew that I was about to get belted, but there was something Sid needed to hear first. I took a deep breath.

'Look, Sid, I'm sorry people used to call you names at school, and I'm sorry that your parents are bullies too. We're all sorry.'

Sid didn't like that.

He came straight at me, pushed me over and yelled down at my face,

'YOU DON'T KNOW NOTHIN'!'

I was left
looking up into
his angry face
and a big fist
and it was
like that
was all there
was that
mattered. It
made me think that
this was the same thing that Sid must
have seen, once upon a time, when he was
taught to be a bully.

Maybe by his parents.

I dragged myself away from his fist and stood
back up.

I looked across at my friends. I didn't know what
to do.

Blocker came over because he knew I was about
to get bashed, only I said, 'No Block, stay there,
this is my problem.'

'We can still fight. I can still fight.'

Blocker was a good friend.

'No, this is my problem.'

If nothing else, I was going to make sure that my
friends didn't get hurt.

I was scared, but there was no running from this. It had to end, somehow.

I said to Sid, 'If you want to bash me, Sid, then bash me, if that will make you feel better.'

Sid rubbed his hands together.

'Well, thank you for the invitation, Tangles. It will make me feel a whole lot better. And what are your friends going to do? Just watch and do nothing?'

I looked over at them all and smiled. I was glad they were here. It was weird. Even though Sid was about to bash me, I didn't mind so much. There was something more important. It was almost as if I wanted him to hit me just to prove that being a bully wasn't going to make me run away and hide anymore.

'No. They're going to watch and feel sorry for you and for your gang who have to follow you.'

Sid pushed me over again.

FIGHT! 'FIGHT! FIGHT! FIGHT! FIGHT! FIGHT! FIGHT! FI GHT!

He pushed me so hard I whacked my head on the ground. Pain blazed through my head and I felt angry at him for hurting me. An urge came on me to jump up and throw punches, but I stopped myself, remembering Tabby's words ... 'Don't fight, whatever you do.'

Getting angry was his way, and would only let him win.

I stood up slowly, saying, 'You don't have to do this, Sid. Vinnie, do you want to be like this? Toddo? Jimmy? We don't respect this, we're just afraid.'

Sid punched me.
I didn't even see it
coming because I was
talking to his gang. I landed
hard on the ground again.

'Now will you shut up?!' growled Sid.

My head was spinning and when I sat up I had to
blink and blink until it stopped.

I touched my nose. There was blood and it really
hurt.

A chant started up. Tabby was leading it.

# Poor Sid, poor bully Sid ...
# Poor Sid, poor bully Sid ...
# Poor Sid, poor bully Sid ...

Sid didn't like it at all.

## He yelled, 'SHUT UP!'

But they didn't, and some called out,

# 'We're not afraid of you!'

I stood up. I had just been punched by Sid. The thing that had scared me so much for weeks had finally happened. And yeah, it hurt and I really wished he hadn't done it, but I was able to stand back up.

I wobbled a bit, but I was a Russian bear.

I said to Sid, 'The hammer breaks glass but it also forges steel.'

Sid looked confused.

I really knew what it meant now.

'Every time you hit me, Sid, I'll get stronger.'

Sid decided to test my words by hitting me again, but he didn't smile like he normally did. He was distracted by everyone chanting.

They were yelling,

**LOSER** and **LONELY LOSER.**

I forced myself up again and called out to everyone, **'Stop! Stop saying that!'**

I was waving my hands and yelling and eventually they stopped. I turned to Sid. He was breathing heavily. His eyes were wild and his nostrils were wide open.

'You don't have to keep doing this, Sid. You don't, and your gang doesn't. Vinnie, Toddo, Jimmy, you don't have to follow Sid. You can just walk away.'

I could taste blood in my mouth as I talked.

Sid didn't answer me. He yelled at his gang instead.

## 'GET 'EM! Why aren't you getting 'em?'

119

Jimmy, Vinnie and Toddo didn't move. They were looking at the ground, or anywhere except at Sid.

I knew why they weren't getting us. I was showing them another way. I was showing them how to be brave. It wasn't enough that I just ask them to walk away, I had to show them.

I rubbed the blood away from my mouth.

'Come on, Sid. This is stupid. Come over to my house, we can all go over there, have some food and hang out.'

# 'AS IF!'

He took another swing at me but missed because he wasn't concentrating.

My mum came running up the street. I heard her yell my name but Mrs Dukarsky popped out from behind a tree, grabbed her elbow and shooshed her.

Everyone was quiet for a second.

I called out, 'Come on, everyone, we'll be Sid's friends, won't we?'

Everyone was saying, 'Yeah,' and, 'We'll be your friends.'

They were saying it to Vinnie, Jimmy and Toddo too.

I really thought Sid might say okay. I really did.

'You're all a bunch of punies!' is what he said. But he didn't seem so large anymore.

He called to his gang, **'Come on, let's go.'**

He jumped on his bike but his gang didn't move.

## 'Come on!'

They shook their heads.

'Nah, we're staying here.'

Sid growled at them.

# 'Get on your bikes or I'll smash youse too!!!'

Jimmy said, 'We don't want to be in your gang no more.'

'Yeah, we aren't afraid of you no more either,' said Vinnie.

Sid glared at them for a while and then rode off.

Even though Sid riding off was like ice cream to my eyes, I honestly felt disappointed that he was leaving. I wondered where he would go. Home to his parents?

Jimmy, Vinnie and Toddo stayed with us. They were a bit awkward at first because they were bigger than us and had been our enemies until about two seconds ago, but Tabby went over and shook their hands and then everyone surrounded them and started cheering.

Mum came running up and gave me a big cuddle, which wasn't too embarrassing because my head hurt heaps and I really wanted her to fix it, especially my nose. But not with Doctor Malvoy because he would probably squeeze it.

Mum whispered to me that she was very proud of me but the next time I wanted to be brave, could I please check with her first.

My friends surrounded me and we were so happy.

I looked across at Tabby and nodded, 'Thanks.'

I also realised right then that I didn't need superpowers to defeat bad things, I just needed friends.

Jessica even came up and asked me if my nose hurt, and when I said yes she stamped on my foot really hard and said, 'Maybe a sore foot will make your nose feel better.'

Then I realised that maybe I could do with some superpowers after all, at least enough for one blast!

Tabby bobbed up and said quietly, 'That was amazing, Freddy. I'm so proud of you.'

That meant a lot to me.

Then she asked really loud,

## 'Who would you rather be, a winner of a fight but have no friends, or the loser of a fight and have heaps of friends?'

Everyone said they wanted to be a loser with friends — even Jimmy, Toddo and Vinnie, and like, they've never lost a fight ever!

Mum invited everyone back to our house for a special afternoon party. She said she was going to make a large bowl of **punch** for everyone to drink, which we all thought was pretty funny.

On the way home I wondered about Sid. I did feel sorry for him, but he was so angry. Maybe we needed to give him more time, maybe another chance.

But that was in the future sometime, because right now we had something else to do.

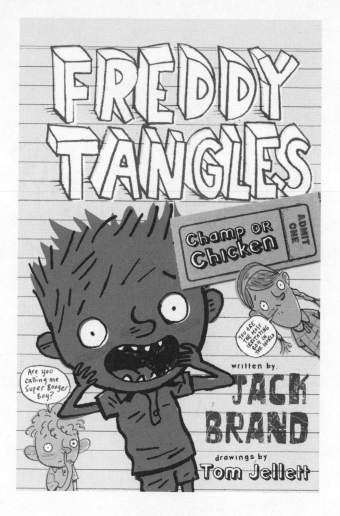

OUT NOW